Sweet Surprises
and other short stories

Stefania Hartley

ALSO AVAILABLE IN
EBOOK AND LARGE PRINT

ISBN: 978-1-914606-71-7

These short stories were first published individually in The People's Friend magazine.

Edited by Sandy Salisbury
Cover by Joseph Witchall
https://josephwitchall.com/

To my readers x

CONTENTS

1 Sweet Surprises 1

2 Room for Renovation 11

3 Good Enough 21

4 A Shy Bride 29

5 At Close Quarters 39

6 Throw in The Towel 50

7 Great Expectations 60

8 Under Her Nose 66

9 The Locked Door 71

10 Pumpkins Everywhere! 79

Other books 89

About the Author 91

1. SWEET SURPRISES

This year, the run-up to Easter had been incredibly busy in Giuliana's *pasticceria*, especially the made-to-order eggs. Easter was in two days and she put the last two surprises in the last two eggs and sealed them. After a thirteen-hour day, she could finally go home and put her feet up.

Tomorrow she would decorate the eggs with sugar flowers, chocolate butterflies and the names of the recipients in her best calligraphy with white chocolate.

She made a note of which egg was which, then turned off the lights and went home.

***

Elio glanced at his girlfriend as he pulled up outside one of the most expensive restaurants in Catania. As expected, her eyebrows shot up.

"Wow, this is a surprise!" she said.

Elio smiled. This was only the first of the surprises he had planned for his girlfriend—

hopefully soon fiancée.

"I hope you don't mind seafood instead of lamb for our Easter lunch," he said.

The April sun glittered on the calm surface of the water like a promise of warmer days to come. A promise of happiness.

"Not at all," she replied enthusiastically.

They were shown to the secluded table with sea view that he had requested especially for the occasion. He had informed the restaurant manager about the special occasion, and the man had assured him that they wouldn't be disturbed with dishes served or taken away at inappropriate times.

The waiters, who were lined up along the entrance corridor, greeted them with smiles that felt particularly warm. A couple also sent encouraging winks to Elio. It was clear that the staff had been informed of his plans to propose at the end of the meal.

"The view is stunning!" Concetta said, taking in the Gulf of Catania that stretched out before them when they were shown to their table.

She praised the oysters starter, complimented the linguine of the first course, and declared that the langoustines of the second course were heavenly.

This was all encouraging for Elio. He had

hardly eaten anything: nerves had locked his stomach.

"I don't think I can fit anything more in," Concetta said.

"But you'll have to have the Easter egg. It's Easter!" Elio said, trying not to panic.

The made-to-order Easter egg he had especially commissioned from the *pasticceria* was the most important part of the meal.

"Oh, yes, I do have space for that!"

At Elio's nod, one of the waiters floated to their table with a beautifully decorated egg on a silver tray.

Concetta's hands flew to her chest. "Elio, it's got our names on! Did you have it made for us?"

"Yes, I did." Elio smiled. "Check out what's inside."

"How can I break something so beautiful?"

"You must." His palms were sweating now.

What if he had got it wrong and she didn't want the surprise he had in store for her? Maybe she thought that things between them were just fine as they were and had no wish to push their relationship up to the next level.

"Only if you want to," he said.

"I do."

She picked up the egg with both hands and tapped it on the shiny silver tray. A small crack appeared. She tapped it again, harder this time, and deeper cracks spread.

Elio felt each one in his bones. Please, say yes. Then, out of the broken egg, peeked… an envelope?

Where was the little velvet box? An engagement ring couldn't fit in an envelope as flat as that one. Was this a joke?

While his mind spun with possibilities—none of them good—she pulled out the envelope and tore it open.

"Two tickets for a football match." Her smiled dropped a little. Neither of them had ever been interested in football.

"Isn't there anything else inside?"

She turned the egg upside down and shook it. "No."

"Oh, blast it. This isn't the surprise you were supposed to get," he said.

"What was it supposed to be?"

How could he tell her like this? This wasn't the way he had planned to propose!

***

Carlo watched a smile spread on Giorgia's face as she took in her name written in curly white chocolate over the fat belly of the Easter egg.

"You had this made for me?" she asked with pleasant surprise.

"Yes."

It had cost a lot more than the usual supermarket egg, but this year it was their fifth anniversary and he wanted to thank her for being a faithful companion, a devoted mother to their children, and… unfortunately, not yet wife.

Heaven only knew how much Carlo wished he could make her his wife, but they couldn't afford a wedding at the moment. At least, not the kind of wedding he knew she wanted: a big white dress, family and friends in attendance, and a meal with many courses and plenty of good wine.

One day, when they had saved up enough money, they'd have that kind of wedding.

Giorgia shook the egg with childish excitement. Something rattled inside, which was strange. The surprise he had asked the *pasticceria* to put inside it was only a paper envelope. Maybe it was a piece of loose chocolate rattling inside.

"There's a surprise inside! You cheeky monkey, how much money did you spend?" she said in mock reproach.

Yes, he had spent a fair bit of money on the football tickets that were inside the egg, but if he couldn't give her the wedding she deserved, at least he should take her out to have some fun.

The football team they supported was coming to town, and he had managed to get tickets for their match. He had been lucky, because they had sold out in minutes. She was going to love this surprise, and he couldn't wait to see her face when she opened the envelope inside the egg.

"What's the surprise, Mummy? Open it!" their children chorused.

"It's too beautiful to break it," Giorgia said.

"You must open it," he said.

"Sorry, egg," she said, then kissed it and hit it against the kitchen table.

Chocolate shrapnel flew in all directions, and out of the belly of the egg tumbled a little parcel. It didn't look anything like the envelope he had given to the shop. Someone had nicked his tickets!

He was about to jump to his feet and take the egg straight back to the shop, but Georgia was now unwrapping the parcel.

Her eyes widened as she took in the small velvet box in her hands. It looked like a jeweller's box.

"You didn't!" she said.

She was right. He didn't. He had no idea what that was.

She looked at the box again and opened it

slowly, almost fearfully.

From where he was, he couldn't see what was inside, but whatever it was, it was making Giorgia's eyes very shiny.

She lifted her gaze up to him and he saw tears about to spill over.

"You kept this very quiet," she said, and her voice caught with emotion.

She lifted a diamond ring out of the box.

Carlo's head spun. That was an engagement ring. Giorgia thought he was proposing. He could tell her that it was a mistake, or he could go along with it and propose. For all these years he had wanted to do just that, so why not? He would sort the money and the practicalities later. It was too late to worry about them when an engagement ring was already in her hands. So he dropped on one knee and took her hand in his.

"Giorgia, will you marry me?" he asked seriously.

"Yes," she answered.

He wiped the tears off her beautiful face and took the ring to put it on her finger.

Oh, no—too small. He mentally rolled his eyes at his own stupidity. How could he have imagined that a stranger's ring would fit?

"I'm sorry, darling," he said.

"It's not a problem. We can get it fixed by

the jeweller or…" She paused, looking a little sheepish. "If you don't mind, we could exchange it for something a little more modest? This one looks like it might have cost more than we can afford."

Quite. Also, he wasn't sure that the ring's rightful owner was willing to sell it, and there was no way that he would keep it without attempting to reunite it with its owner first.

Giorgia looked straight into his eyes. "And please promise that we won't spend crazy money on a silly big wedding either."

"I thought you wanted a big fairy-tale wedding."

She laughed. "When I was younger, yes. But now I'd rather spend the money on a family holiday or a kitchen extension. Wouldn't you?"

Carlo sighed with relief. They could afford a ring and a wedding after all. If only they'd had this conversation sooner!

Tomorrow he'd buy her a new engagement ring and return the strangers' ring to the *pasticceria*… But not before demanding his football tickets back!

***

Elio felt like the wind hadn't just gone out of his sail, but out of his lungs too.

"I'm sorry, Concetta. There must have been a switch over at the *pasticceria*."

He ran a hand over his face. If only he could make himself disappear!

She put her hand over his arm. "Don't worry. It doesn't matter."

"I appreciate your attempt to cheer me up, but unfortunately, it does matter. You don't know what the surprise was."

She smiled. "I think I do."

"How?"

"Expensive restaurant, extra-friendly waiters, secluded table… but even if that hadn't made me suspicious, your nerves gave it away."

Now it was Elio's turn to be surprised.

"But you don't need be nervous, because by the time a girl has got into the restaurant or whatever you have organised when you want to propose, she's already decided what she'll answer. And I bet most girls wouldn't have come if they were going to turn you down."

"Do you mean…"

"Oh, no. You can't take a shortcut like this, making me say yes without asking the question," she said with a cheeky smile. "The ring doesn't matter to me, but being asked properly does."

He smiled at her honesty and spirit. They were some of the reasons why he had fallen in love with her.

He pushed back his chair and kneeled in front of her.

"Will you marry me, Concetta?"

"Yes, I will."

Cheering exploded from the waiters who had kept themselves at a distance, following the scene. The bubbly was popped and everyone joined in a toast.

***

It was Easter Monday, and Giuliana was surprised to find two customers waiting in front of her shop before eight o'clock. Wasn't Easter over? If this week turned out as busy as the last, she was going to have a tantrum.

She entered from the back door, turned on the lights, put on her apron and finally walked to the glass doors to unlock them.

To her surprise, the two men didn't pay her any attention. Instead, they exchanged some parcels, laughing.

"Good morning. You can come in," she said, opening the doors.

"Thanks, but we're done."

They shook hands, exchanged wishes and walked away.

Giuliana shrugged and went to the back of the shop to prepare the few leftover Easter eggs for sale.

2. ROOM FOR RENOVATION

"The café is closing for renovations tomorrow," Tanino told his wife as soon as he entered the kitchen. Then he heaved a sigh and slumped into his chair.

Melina was so discombobulated that she put pepper in the bubbling tomato sauce instead of salt. "For how long?"

"Four weeks."

Good heavens! What were Tanino and his friends going to do with themselves for all that time?

"Carmelo's café doesn't need any renovations; it's perfect as it is!"

"How would you know? You never go."

This was true. It was a dingy shop with rickety chairs and stained tables, mostly frequented by men like Tanino and his friends. They spent every morning there, drinking coffee and playing scopa cards.

"I've been once, when I was out with our

granddaughter and she needed the toilet urgently. So, will you and your friends meet at the other café, at the end of the street?"

"No way! We'll never give our custom to Carmelo's competition. We just won't meet for four weeks. Anyway, Rocco is going to visit his daughter in Milan, Vincenzo is taking his wife on holiday and Luigi is going to help his son paint his flat."

"And what are you going to do?" she asked.

"I'll find something." He sighed.

Melina shivered. When Tanino was newly retired, before he started frequenting the café, he had rattled around their flat like a lone coin in a piggybank. One day she'd returned home from the market and found all the plant pots on the balcony rearranged in order of size, regardless of the plants in them.

Another time she found the entire contents of her kitchen cupboards lined up in alphabetical order, so that the pasta sat uncomfortably next to the *patatine* crisps, the couscous rubbed shoulders with the chocolate and the lentils were improbably partnered with the liquorice. It took Melina most of an hour to find the carton of milk which wasn't under "L" for latte, milk, but under "U" for UHT.

She shuddered at the thought of what Tanino might get up to if he stayed at home for one entire month.

"Why don't you help Carmelo keep an eye on the builders—watch over the works and make sure they do a proper job?" she suggested.

"That's a great idea," Tanino said.

***

The lift was broken. Melina had no choice but to climb the three flights of stairs to her flat.

Adjusting her shopping bags on the crook of her elbows to balance the weight, Melina set off, regretting buying a watermelon and two kilos of tomatoes.

By the time she completed the first flight of stairs, she had to stop to rest her leg, which was playing up.

The flowerpot on the windowsill of the landing caught her gaze.

It was decorated with the symbol of Sicily—a triskelion three-legged gorgon's head.

"I could do with an extra leg," she thought to herself.

In fact, it was only eleven o'clock and she had already taken the dog for a walk, queued at the post office, dropped her shoes at the cobbler's, shopped at the market and stopped by the baker's.

Her arms had been so full that the baker had

left the counter and stuffed the bread into one of the bags so that she didn't have to put them down. By the time she reached her flat, sweat beaded her top lip but she had no free hands to wipe it off.

She was wondering whether she could fish the house keys out of her bag with her teeth when the door opened wide and Tanino stood before her.

"I heard you come up the stairs." He registered the shopping bags hanging off Melina's arms. "Why didn't you call me? I would have come down and helped you."

Melina didn't answer. All her brain's processing power was taken by the sight of her husband wearing a newspaper hat and wielding a trowel.

"What's going on? What are you up to?"

"Come and see." He smiled smugly.

A bucket of fresh mortar sat on the kitchen floor.

"The builders at the café had some left over so they let me take it home. Look, I've replaced the broken tile."

Melina's heart sank. The missing tile under the foot of the kitchen cupboard made it just short enough for her to reach the top shelf. Now it was back to being too high for her.

She forced out a polite smile and Tanino

rubbed his hands.

"I knew you'd be pleased! I still have some mortar left. It'll harden soon so, is there anything else you'd like me to repair?"

Melina slumped on a chair. She was hungry, tired and had only just enough energy to cook lunch in a tidy kitchen.

Instead, there were trowels scattered on the counters and buckets of fresh mortar to dodge.

She glanced out sullenly at the balcony and something about her flowerpots grabbed her attention.

"What…?"

Tanino grinned. "You often complain that the wind blows your plants over so I've cemented the pots to the floor."

She held her head between her hands. "I was only away for a couple of hours…"

***

It was impossible to be cross with Tanino because he always acted with the best intentions.

Even when he made the shower curtain so short that it stuck to your body when you showered, changed the light bulbs to ones that gave out a horrid blue glare and moved the microwave so far from the kitchen counter that she was in danger of dropping heavy dishes on the floor. Melina was exhausted.

Three more weeks before the café reopened. She had no idea how to keep her husband at bay for all that time.

She had just lain down on the sofa to rest her leg after clearing up lunch when their little dog, Bello, tottered up to her and nuzzled her hand with his lead in his mouth.

Melina sighed. "Oh, sweetie, can you please let me rest a little longer?"

Bello dropped the lead into her hand and gave her a puppy-eyed look.

"Why don't you ask Tanino? He's got energy to spare," Melina joked.

Much to her surprise, Bello picked up his lead and tottered out of the room. He's not going to have much luck, she thought. Tanino was asleep.

But soon after, Tanino appeared at the threshold with Bello's lead in his hand and the bleary eyes of a man woken up in the middle of a nap.

"Bello seems to want me to take him for a walk. Do you mind?"

He sounded as flattered as he was surprised.

"If he's chosen you…" Melina shrugged, as if she was totally innocent.

When Tanino and Bello returned from their walk, Tanino was full of excitement.

"Guess what, Melina? I met an old classmate

of mine at the public villa. He has a dog, too, and tomorrow we are meeting at the same time—if you don't mind me taking Bello for a walk again."

"Not at all. Why don't you take Bello for his morning walk too?"

"Sure. I've got nothing else to do."

"And as you're out, could you pop over to the market and buy something for lunch? And buy bread from the baker's? My shoes also need collecting from the cobbler, but it's on your way."

The next day, Tanino returned home at eleven o'clock with a full grocery shop. When he left the house again with Bello to meet his old school friend at the public villa, Melina stretched on the sofa with a book and put her leg up.

By supper time, her leg didn't hurt at all and she felt as fresh as a bun just out of the baker's oven. By giving Tanino her errands, she had—as the Italian saying goes—caught two birds with one bean. Tanino was too busy to get up to any DIY mischief at home and her leg was healing fast.

She remembered the three-legged woman's head, symbol of the Sicilian island. She had finally got the third leg she needed. It was Tanino!

***

"Sorry, Melina, but I can't walk Bello today. The café is reopening."

"But… I've got a hair appointment!"

And Melina had promised a phone call to her sister, and she wanted to finish a book…

"I'm sorry, but I can't miss the café's reopening party. I can do the grocery shop on the way home, though."

Having Tanino be her extra leg had been wonderful, but now Melina had better get used to just having a hand from him instead.

When Tanino returned home for lunch, singing the praises of the renovated café, Melina's curiosity flared up like a bonfire. So the following morning she took Bello on a different walk which went right past the café.

New wrought-iron tables spilled onto the pavement, shaded by a cheerful yellow and white awning. A multicoloured palette of artisan ice cream trays was displayed right by the entrance so that you didn't have to go deep into the shop to buy one.

"Melina, hello! Come and join us," Melina's friends called from one of the tables. They, too, had come to inspect the new café where their husbands spent every morning.

Hours went by as they chatted and Melina was taken by surprise when, around twelve o'clock, she saw Tanino and his friends filing out of the back of the shop.

"Good heavens, I should be home making lunch!" Melina exclaimed, jumping to her feet.

Tanino spotted her and the surprise on his face turned into a smile.

"Melina, do you like it? Come, see how nice it is!"

He didn't seem even a little worried that his lunch was going to be late, so she followed him in.

The walls were now pastel yellow. Strategically placed mirrors made the place look airy and more luminous, and the new indoor tables and chairs were sparkling clean.

"Carmelo has done a sterling job," she said.

The man himself waddled out from behind the till and came to meet her.

"Have you come to admire your husband's work?"

"My husband's work?"

"Don't you know? He helped me choose the new tiles, the paints, the fittings. He said that we needed lighter, friendlier colours to attract women and children too"—he lowered his voice conspiratorially—"but I think that who he really wanted to attract was you. And hasn't he done a good job?"

Melina whipped her head round to Tanino.

"You did this? For me?"

Tanino scratched the back of his neck, looking shy, while Carmelo confirmed it.

"He's been wonderful, and not just for the renovation. He helps me choose suppliers, check invoices, deal with paperwork…"

When she'd imagined him spending the mornings playing cards and drinking coffee with his friends, he was also helping running the café!

No wonder he had been so helpful to her once he stopped going.

"I offered him to become my business partner," Carmelo continued, "but he said no. Many times I asked him to stay for lunch on me, but he always said that he couldn't let you eat alone. But now that you're here, Melina, can I offer you both lunch?"

It sounded like the perfect solution. "Yes, please!"

The following day the offer was repeated.

"Even if you had lunch here every day of the week, I'd still be in debt towards Tanino so, please, let me treat you."

They accepted and from then on Melina didn't have to carry any more bags of shopping. For their supper, they shopped on the way home, and Tanino always carried the bags.

3. GOOD ENOUGH

As a young mother before the war, Maria Pia had learnt that the world was full of snares. Everyone looked after their own interests, so outside her immediate family, she trusted nobody and nothing.

And now that the war had finally ended, she was wary of everyone and everything. At the market and in shops she checked her change twice. Before buying eggs, she turned them over, one by one, to check they weren't cracked. If anyone asked her anything in the street, she never stopped to reply.

One day, her husband Mimmo came home. "I met Ciro Piccotta," he told her, "and he asked what our plans are for Raffaella. His brother is looking for a wife for his son."

"Is this the brother who emigrated to America?" Maria Pia asked.

"Yes. They've opened a bakery in New York and they're doing very well."

"If they're doing so well, can't they find a wife for their son over there?"

"The young man wants to marry a girl from his parents' village," Mimmo explained. "He came over to Sicily with the American troops during the war and fell in love with our land and our people. His parents have enquired with their family here, and Ciro has put forward Raffaella's name."

"It sounds fishy to me," Maria Pia replied.

"Who would you rather she married?" He rolled his eyes. "Most of the young men in our village struggle to scrape a living. America is the land of milk and honey. This might be the best marriage offer our daughter will get."

"If Raffaella likes him, I won't say no." Maria Pia sighed.

***

The negotiations between the families started and a photo of the young man arrived through the post. Raffaella's parents, grandparents, uncles and aunts were all gathered to see it.

Angelino Piccotta had a friendly face and intelligent eyes, and Raffaella immediately liked him.

"A fine young man," an auntie said.

"Looks robust enough," an uncle agreed.

But her mother frowned. "Why is he

wearing a hat?" she asked. "Has he got a head injury?"

"Maybe he's bald," an auntie suggested.

Raffaella didn't mind if he was bald or hairy, so long as he was going to be a good husband. His kind eyes seemed to suggest he might be.

"For all we know," Mum began, folding her arms, "he could have had part of his skull blown off by a bomb. I'm not having a husband who's missing part of his head for my daughter."

"Then we'll ask for a photo without a hat," Dad ruled.

The next photo that came through the post was a close-up headshot. This time, Angelino wasn't wearing a hat, and showed off a luxuriant shock of shiny black hair.

Raffaella liked him a lot, especially as the photo came with a letter where he expressed his wish to correspond with her.

"He's all right," one of the uncles said.

"He's better than all right," one of the aunts retorted.

"Is he good enough, Maria Pia?" Dad asked Mum.

But Mum's lips remained pursed. "The first photo was half-length. This one is a headshot," she pointed out. "They never send us a full-length photo. I reckon he's lost his legs in the war."

"Maybe they don't send us a full-length photo because it's expensive," Grandma reasoned. "By asking for all these photos we're making them spend a fortune."

"Then they're money-pinchers," Mum argued. "We don't want our daughter to marry into a family of money-pinchers."

"Better than marrying a spendthrift or a gambler," one of the aunties pointed out.

Her husband was known for losing all his weekly wages at the cards before he even got home.

"Maybe they're just careful with money," Grandma suggested.

"We'll ask for another photo," Dad ruled again.

When the new photo arrived, it was another headshot, but taken from a different angle. This time, Angelino's mop of hair was oiled and slicked back, and he looked more seriously into the camera.

It looked as if the Piccottas were trying to tick the required boxes but without any idea what these might be. But they were certainly ticking Raffaella's boxes, because she was getting more and more smitten with Angelino.

"His legs are not in the photo," her mother complained once again. "I was right—he's lost his legs in the war."

"If he's got a bakery, he won't need his legs too much," one of the aunties said. "He can mix dough sitting down or work at the till."

That auntie had varicose veins and had learnt to do most of her chores sitting down.

"Why should my daughter go all the way to America to marry a man without legs, when there are young men with all their limbs here in the village?" Mum asked.

But Raffaella didn't mind whether he had legs or not. She had read his letters and had fallen in love.

"Then let's ask them specifically for a full body photo," an auntie said.

"Not after we've already requested two photos," an uncle retorted.

"The young man will have to come over a little before the wedding," Grandma piped up. "It will be obvious then if he has legs or not."

The marriage was agreed and preparations started.

***

When the Piccotas got off the bus, it was clear that Angelino had two working legs.

Maria Pia felt a naughty prick of disappointment but pushed it away and smiled at her future in-laws instead.

Her husband invited the Piccottas to their

home, where the last details of the nuptials were discussed. While Maria Pia grilled the Piccottas, the bride- and groom-to-be sat in silence on the sofa at a respectable distance, sending furtive glances to each other.

But that evening, as the Piccottas left, Maria Pia watched them walk away.

"Angelino's gait is a little stiff," she said to her husband.

"So is his parents'," Mimmo replied. "It was a long walk from the bus stop to our house. The Americans aren't as used to walking as we are. They travel everywhere by car."

"But why is Angelino wearing long trousers?" Maria Pia pressed on.

"Because he's not a child anymore," Mimmo returned.

"Or is it to hide a wooden leg?"

Mimmo finally sighed in exasperation. "I'm not going to ask him to show us what's under his trousers, if that's what you're thinking."

But nobody had to resort to that. The next morning, when Maria Pia went to the harbour to buy fish from the fishermen, Angelino was quay-jumping with the local lads, and there was absolutely nothing amiss with his legs.

***

On the day of the wedding, the guests were already filling the pews, and the groom was standing at the front of the church, looking nervous and excited.

But there was no sign of the bride.

"What's the matter, Raffaella?" Maria Pia asked through her daughter's bedroom door.

"I'm scared," the girl answered between sobs.

Guilt suddenly crushed Maria Pia. She had piled so many suspicions and doubts on the groom that she'd managed to shatter her daughter's affection for him and her resolve to marry him.

Hand on heart, could she really say that she had only acted out of due diligence? Or had she tried to find faults in Angelino and America for fear of losing her daughter? Every time she thought of the ship that would take Raffaella away to America, her heart sank like the *Titanic.*

Was it better to have her daughter at home with her, but sad and lonely, or to know her happy beyond the ocean?

"His legs are fine. I've seen him dive from the end of the quay," Maria Pia confessed.

"But he could still turn out to be a bad husband," Raffaella cried.

"Angelino seems a good man."

"But how can I be sure?"

"Nobody can be sure about anything," Maria Pia reasoned. "Marriage is a risk, like most things in life. We can never completely protect ourselves from harm. Just look out the window now. Our family lives under a volcano. In life, the only safe place is the coffin."

Raffaella then opened her door with tear-stricken cheeks and smiled. "I think I'm ready to go."

***

Raffaella found that New York was full of Sicilians. She could get by without knowing much English, but she quickly learnt it anyway and made friends with other immigrants who had come from all over the world.

She loved the bakery and, as she was pregnant with one child after another, she sat at the till taking payment and chatting to customers, while Angelino worked in the kitchen and behind the counter.

For every new baby that was born, she sent a photo to her mum and dad. And her husband never knew why she always insisted that they were full-length photos.

4. A SHY BRIDE

It was a first for Don Pericle. He usually hosted wedding receptions in his ancestral home, Villa Lingualarga, but on this occasion the couple had asked him to host the civil ceremony too.

He already felt that it was a privilege to host the most significant party in the couple's lives. Hosting the wedding itself filled him with even more gratitude and pleasure. He had seen hundreds of couples in almost forty years as a wedding organiser, but he remembered each and every one. This couple, the first to pronounce their vows under his roof, would be especially remembered.

The hundred guests were filing into the grand ballroom, which was all decked out with pink peonies matching the blush pink velvet curtains.

The town's mayor was already there, with a shiny green, white and red sash draped across her chest. The groom was there too, ashen and beaded with sweat, tapping his leg on the floor like a woodpecker against the bark of a tree.

"Great suit, Antonio." Don Pericle patted the groom on the shoulder encouragingly.

"Thank you. Don Pericle, I can't stop shaking. I keep imagining the worst things. What if she's changed her mind?"

"None of that is going to happen, Antonio. Rosanna is smitten with you."

A whisper rippled across the room. The guests sitting nearer to the balcony had heard the bride's car grind gravel and spotted it pulling into the villa's car park.

"She's here," Don Pericle told the groom, who grinned with relief.

Don Pericle positioned himself at the room's threshold so that he could signal to the musician to play the wedding march when he saw the bride turn into the corridor.

But minutes passed, and the bride never did.

***

All right, she hadn't slept the whole night and she'd been off her food from the evening before, but overall Rosanna had managed to keep her nerves under control. That was until she got out of the car.

The notes of the violins wafting out of Villa Lingualarga's terrace had attracted her attention and, through the open windows, she had seen the guests.

So many people, all there for her and Antonio! They had dressed up, some had travelled a long way and others had bought new outfits for the occasion. Would she be able to deliver the show that they were expecting?

Memories from her past made her shudder. Her first and only ballet performance where, before the eyes of all the other children and their parents, she had tripped on stage. What if she messed up again? What if this show didn't live up to the guests' expectations?

All she wanted was to become Antonio's wife.

"You are shaking, darling. Calm down," her father told her as she took his arm and got out of the car.

"I c-can't," she stuttered, her teeth chattering.

"You're going to bite Antonio when it's time for the kiss if you don't stop."

Instead of releasing the tension, Dad's joke just gave her one more thing to worry about. What if Antonio didn't like her in her wedding dress? She had never worn anything like it.

She could barely recognise herself with all the make-up that the beautician had put on her. Would Antonio recognise her?

Each step of the grand baroque staircase felt

like a mountain, adding to her breathlessness and dizziness with the increasing altitude.

"My head is spinning, Dad," she murmured once they reached the top.

"We'd better take you to the restroom and you can splash some water on your face," he said.

He, too, sounded tense now.

"Yes, please," she wheezed.

The notes of the violins rang in her ears.

She dived into the restroom as if it was a hurricane-proof shelter. She ran the cold tap, the gushing water drowning the sound to the violins, and she splashed her face. That stopped her from fainting, but as soon as she saw the effect of the water on her make-up, her anxiety grew.

Tears mingled with the tap water. Her mascara had streaked her face with Pierrot tears. She made her cheeks sore by rubbing them with toilet paper. Then the hiccups started. Oh, dear, she was a real mess.

She couldn't walk into the hall like this. It was full of all the people who mattered most to her and Antonio. She glanced at the clock on the wall. How long would it be before someone came looking for her? Her heart went out to Antonio, who was waiting for her under everyone's gaze.

The more she thought about him, the more she felt guilty and the more tears streamed out of her eyes, washing away the last drops of courage she had.

She had no choice but to hide there until all the guests had gone home.

***

"Is everything all right, Don Pericle?" Antonio asked.

It was a very good question. At least five minutes had passed and the bride still hadn't appeared.

It didn't take that long to walk up the staircase, through the corridor and round the corner where he could see her.

"I'm sure it is, but I'll check."

Antonio grabbed his arm and looked into his eyes. "Don Pericle, do you think she's changed her mind?"

"Highly unlikely," he replied soberly. "She probably has a problem with her dress or her shoes, or her hairdo has come undone."

Antonio let out the breath that he was holding. "I hope so."

Don Pericle strode down the corridor towards the restroom. The bride's father was waiting outside. The look on his face didn't bode well.

"Rosanna got a little shaky on the way up the

stairs," the man explained.

Don Pericle suddenly remembered their wedding planning meetings. Rosanna had mentioned that she hated attention and she had joked that she might faint when she walked down the aisle. At the time, he had taken it as a joke, but now it struck him that she maybe meant it literally. How careless of him!

"Is anyone with her?" he asked her father.

The man shook his head. "I couldn't call her mother without walking into the hall and alarming everyone."

"We certainly don't want to do that." Pericle nodded. "Then it's up to one of us to help her."

The man glanced uncertainly at the silhouette of a lady etched on the door.

"I fear that my nerves might make hers worse."

Pericle noticed the man's trembling hands. "Quite. Then, if you will allow me to comfort your daughter...?"

"Please."

***

Rosanna was hiding in one of the cubicles when she heard the door open and someone walk in, doubtlessly looking for her.

It hadn't taken as long as she had imagined. She hoped it was her mum or Antonio. She very much owed him an apology.

"Rosanna? May I see you?"

She recognised Don Pericle's voice. It wasn't too bad: she had grown fond of him and admired his kindness and wisdom. Surely he could pass a message on to Antonio.

"Don Pericle, I'm sorry. I can't do it,' she cried, bursting out of the cubicle.

He scanned her, taking in her puffy eyes and smeared make-up, then pulled her into his arms, where she burst into tears once more until most of her tension had drained out and she was left with gentle hiccups.

"Which part can't you do? Marrying Antonio or walking into a room full of people?" he asked her soothingly.

"I want to marry Antonio more than anything! I just can't walk into that room with all the people watching me."

"Then there's no problem." Don Pericle smiled and offered her his handkerchief.

It smelled of lavender. She held onto that warm scent as an antidote to all the jagged thoughts spinning in her head.

He walked pensively to the window that looked out onto the garden.

"We'll send everyone away," he declared.

"We can't do that after all the trouble they've gone to."

"They won't mind if we give them a lovely

concert in the garden, which I'm sure the string quartet will be happy to improvise. Meanwhile, you and Antonio will get married upstairs and can join them afterwards."

"But our families will never forgive us if we don't let them attend the actual wedding," she objected.

Don Pericle scratched his salt and pepper beard.

"Okay. You and Antonio must discuss your options. If I send everyone else into the garden, will you come out and talk to him?"

"Yes, I will."

"Good. Then wait here and I'll come back when the coast is clear and you can come out."

Rosanna wiped her eyes. "Thank you so much, Don Pericle."

***

Antonio waited in the big empty ballroom with his best friend, Paolo, and Rosanna's sister, Gigliola.

Don Pericle hadn't allowed anyone else in the room. All the better, perhaps: if Rosanna was going to call off the wedding, he wouldn't like their break-up to be any more public than that.

A moment later, Rosanna burst flying down the hall like a vision, enveloped in a cloud of white tulle, curls breaking free from the bun, longing etched on her face.

His heart leaped. Her heels echoed in the empty hall to the same rhythm as his heart. Perhaps she wasn't going to break up with him after all.

"Antonio!"

She hurtled into his arms. Her poor face bore the signs of the anguish she must have been through. He squeezed her tight and held her tighter, as if in doing so he could stop her spinning away from him, lost forever.

"I'm so sorry, I wasn't brave enough to face all the people. But I want you to be my husband, Antonio, more than anything in the world. I want to love and cherish you all the days of my life, for better, for worse, for richer, for poorer, in sickness and in health, till the day we die!"

A knot of emotion formed in his throat.

"That's great, because I want you to be my wife, I want to love and cherish you for better, for worse, for richer, for poorer, in sickness and in health, till we die," he rasped.

Don Pericle, who had followed Rosanna into the room, cleared his throat.

"Do I understand correctly that you, Rosanna, want to marry Antonio?"

"Yes!"

"And you, Antonio, want to marry

Rosanna?"

"Double sure!"

"Then…" Slowly and deliberately, Don Pericle pulled a tricolour sash out of his pocket and draped it across his chest.

Rosanna's eyes widened.

"As the mayor has delegated me, and given that your witnesses are here…"

Paolo and Gigliola grinned.

"…I declare you husband and wife."

Don Pericle pulled the marriage registry from under the table and offered Rosanna the special pen.

Rosanna burst into happy tears and hugged Antonio, then they each signed the big book, followed by Paolo and Gigliola.

At that point, there was some ruffling and shuffling behind one of the big heavy velvet curtains, and the mayor tottered out, followed by Rosanna and Antonio's immediate family.

They all started clapping.

Rosanna gasped. "Oh, Don Pericle, thank you!"

Don Pericle smiled. "Now, let the party begin!"

5. AT CLOSE QUARTERS

Veronica and Giuseppe Rossetti were very pleased with their new holiday villa. It had a large garden, a beautiful terrace from which they could see the Tyrrhenian Sea, and plenty of space for parties, like the housewarming party they were having today.

"A toast to Veronica and Giuseppe's new villa!" the guests suggested.

Giuseppe got the bubbly ready, then tinkled his glass for silence.

"Thank you all for coming here tonight. We're so lucky to have found this place. We just fell in love with the view and the silence. It's so quiet here that you can even hear the sea." He paused to allow everyone to appreciate the gentle sloshing of the sea.

Instead, a powerful bray broke the silence. Hee-haw! It was the neighbour's donkey.

Everyone—except Giuseppe and Veronica—burst into laughter.

***

Lia was blissfully asleep in her new villa, dreaming about the bougainvillea and the hibiscus she was going to plant in her new garden.

A noise pulled her back to consciousness. Cock-a-doodle-doo! Her neighbour's cockerel.

Surrounded by all the new villas, that small farmer had clung onto his land like a barnacle to a rock.

What time was it? Six o'clock! Had nobody told the creature that holidaymakers didn't want to get up so early?

The bird gave her just enough time to fall asleep again, then let out another one of his angry calls.

She covered her ears with her pillow, but the cockerel's voice pierced through it.

Lia abandoned her bed and padded to the kitchen. She put the percolator on the hob and waited for the coffee aroma to fill the air and start waking her up.

But instead of the scent of coffee, a stench of goat and sheep wafted in through the French doors.

This was the last straw! She must talk to the farmer. She downed her coffee, got dressed and stormed out of her gate.

***

Pippo scattered seeds for his hens and his cockerel, and smiled at his little flock. Since his wife had passed away, his animals were his only family.

Every morning, when the Sicilian sun painted the sky pink, he got out of bed and fed his donkey and his ponies, his goats and his sheep, his hens and his cockerel, and they thanked him with cheerful clucks, sturdy brays, happy neighs and languorous bleats.

He would never understand how his neighbours could sell their land and their animals. The developers had offered to buy Pippo's land, but he refused, even when they doubled their offer. He could never sell his animals! They needed him, and he needed them.

He was about to go in for his own breakfast, when someone called from the gate.

"Hi! I'm your neighbour on this side." The woman in a flowy dress pointed to the new villa on his right. "Can I have a word with you?"

Pippo walked to the gate.

"Every morning your cockerel crows and wakes me up. Can you stop him?"

"Crowing is what cockerels do," Pippo replied, mystified by the request.

"But I don't want to be woken up at dawn."

How was Pippo to silence his cockerel? And

if he did, how would he know when to get up? Pippo had never owned an alarm clock.

"Also," the woman continued, "the smell of your goats and sheep puts me off my breakfast. Could you take them somewhere else?"

Pippo was confused. His cockerel, his sheep and his goats had been there all along. Why had she built her home there if she didn't want to live next to them?

"Or, perhaps, could you just stop them smelling?" she said, as he was silent.

At that, he concluded that the woman was batty and there was no point trying to reason with her.

"I will make my cockerel be quiet and my goats smell better," he said.

The woman smiled, thanked him and left.

***

A week later, Lia was still being woken up by the cockerel, and the goats and sheep didn't smell better. She concluded that more decisive action was needed.

She paid a visit to the farmer's neighbours on the other side and was pleased to find that the Rossettis were as disgruntled about the nuisance as she was. The three of them resolved to take action together, and made enquiries with solicitors.

The first one told them—politely—that they

should have considered the existence of the farm before buying their homes.

The second one explained that, if they demonstrated that the noise pollution exceeded the legal limit, they would have a case. Unfortunately, the noise survey could only be conducted by the relevant authorities, and their waiting list stretched beyond the end of the summer holidays. They would have to endure the animals all through that summer.

But the third solicitor promised that there wasn't much that a scary solicitor's letter wouldn't solve, and he could help them with that.

They chose the third one.

***

Pippo opened the letter. It wasn't handwritten, so it couldn't be a personal letter. It didn't have numbers, so it couldn't be a bill. And it had no red writing, so it wasn't a final warning.

He concluded that it must be junk mail, so there was no point in taking it to his friend to read it for him. So Pippo tore it up and tossed it on the straw that he used as bedding for his animals.

***

Lia couldn't believe her eyes. She could see through the fence that, just on the other side of her wall, the solicitor's letter, for which they had paid handsomely, lay in pieces under a goat's bottom.

There could have been no clearer message from their neighbour: this was how little he cared about their legal threats.

She rushed to the Rossettis to decide their next course of action.

Threats didn't scare the man. Legal routes would be too slow, and the outcome wasn't guaranteed. Money didn't work: the developer had offered plenty to buy the land, but the farmer hadn't sold.

They had to take matters into their own hands.

***

Giuseppe and Veronica considered muzzling the donkey but concluded that the execution would be difficult. Also, the farmer would eventually notice.

If they couldn't keep the donkey's mouth shut, then they would keep it full.

Every time the donkey brayed, they would throw a carrot at him. With his mouth full, the animal would not bray.

They did this a few times, and on one occasion the carrot hit him on the head, so he brayed even more. But all the other times, the carrot was a good way to silence him. As soon as the donkey made a nuisance of himself, they threw a carrot at him.

Their aim got quite good now, and they didn't need to look at where he was. They could tell from the sound.

But as the number of carrots they had to buy increased, and the donkey brayed more and more, Veronica and Giuseppe realised that their strategy had backfired: by rewarding him with a treat, they were encouraging him to bray more.

***

Lia's plan was simple: if the farmer wouldn't keep his sheep pen nice and clean, she would.

Armed with a bucket of diluted bleach, she approached the wall that separated her garden from the farmer's pen. She snuck her arm through the bars of the fence and reached down on the other side.

As she scrubbed away, she had to admit to herself that the smell of bleach wasn't much more pleasant than that of the animals.

Something was sizzling. Oh no, the stones were frothing!

She swapped the bleach for antibacterial spray. It was a lot more expensive, but at least it smelled of lavender and roses and she could also spray it on the wool of any sheep or goat that wandered within reach.

In no time, the bottle was empty and, the following day, the smell of sheep and goats returned.

Lia bought another bottle and set off to work again. She tied the bottle onto a broom handle and connected the trigger to a string so that she could spray further into the pen.

She had sprayed everything she could reach and was about to pull back, when she felt eyes on the back of her head. She looked cautiously around.

A hen was watching her from her geranium bed, squashing her plants.

"Shoo!" Lia shouted.

The bird clucked, jumped onto the wall and squeezed between the bars of the fence back to her farm.

As long as the gaps in the fence were wide enough for Lia's arm to fit through, they would also be wide enough for the hen. If Lia cared about her geraniums, she would have to give up access to the sheep pen. She went to the shop, bought chicken wire and plastered it over the fence.

With all the kerfuffle, Lia was running late with her daughter's birthday surprise: a swan-shaped meringue.

Lia counted twenty eggs, weighed the sugar and turned on the oven. Then she started cracking the eggs—yolk in one bowl, white in another.

Now and then, a yolk broke and contaminated the white, and she had to discard them and take a new egg from the fridge.

She was cracking the last egg, when a foul smell burst out of the shell. That egg was definitely off.

Lia threw it away and went to the fridge. She was out of eggs!

She needed one more but had no time to go to the shops. Then she remembered. She ran into her garden, and there, under her squashed geraniums, was an egg!

***

It was a hot night but Giuseppe would never sleep with the air conditioner, and Veronica would never sleep with the fan.

Eventually they agreed to sleep with the windows open. They locked downstairs, got into bed, and fell asleep.

In the middle of the night, suddenly a powerful bray woke them up with a start. They groaned and turned to go back to sleep, but the animal continued braying desperately.

The cockerel joined in, the sheep and the goats bleated in response, and soon the entire farm was making a terrible din. No way could anyone sleep through that!

"Please, make them stop!" Veronica begged.

Giuseppe dragged himself to the window with the intention of throwing a slipper at the animals and found himself face-to-face with a stranger.

"Thief!" Giuseppe shouted.

The thief almost lost his footing, scrambled down the terracotta rainwater drainpipe, and crash-landed on the oleander bush. Then he jumped over the fence and ran off.

The donkey stopped braying, the cockerel stopped crowing, the sheep and the goats stopped bleating. Calm was restored.

***

Pippo woke up tired. What a terrible night he'd had! The animals had made a din.

Pippo had had to go out and calm them down. He had searched the farm for foxes or something else that might have caused the upset, but hadn't found anything. Maybe his neighbours had been right to complain about his animals.

A horrible thought came to his mind. After last night, his neighbours could report him for the disturbance his animals had caused!

He was turning these fears around in his mind when someone called from the gate. It was his neighbours. They must have come to complain.

He plodded to the gate and was surprised to see them smiling.

The woman next door handed him an egg-shaped meringue wrapped in paper. "This is for you, to thank you because your hen saved the day for me yesterday."

"And this is for your donkey, to thank him for his timely intervention last night," the couple from the other side said, handing him a bunch of carrots tied with a golden ribbon.

Pippo was confused but he thanked them all and watched them walk back to their homes. And from that day, he didn't receive any more complaints about his animals.

6. THROW IN THE TOWEL

Gregorio admits that there are kind women in the world, but his experience has convinced him that they must be a minority.

So he doesn't hold any hope of every finding a soulmate, and lives by the motto "better alone than in bad company".

Unfortunately, there are some practical difficulties with going through life on his own. For example, there's no one to look after his clothes when he goes for a swim at the beach.

But Gregorio loves Mondello beach too much to wait for his friends to organise a trip there.

So he wears his shabbiest clothes, takes his oldest beach towel—the one with the print of cartoon fish—and he goes on his own.

***

After months of arguing with her boyfriend over the domestic chores, Alessia is single again and intending to remain so.

The experience has convinced her that men are selfish, lazy slobs, and she's better off on her own.

Now that she's done all the crying and self-commiserating her mum and her friends could tolerate, they've sent her to the beach in the hope that she will recover her zest for life.

Unfortunately, none of them can go with her, so Alessia packs her towel and water bottle and sets off on her own.

***

When he finally reaches the beach, Gregorio is hot, sweaty and desperate for a swim. He stretches out his towel on the sand, drops his phone into a plastic bag and hides it under the towel, then piles his shoes and clothes neatly by his towel. Finally, he puts his glasses on top of the pile and heads to the water.

***

Alessia finds the beach crowded, hot and dazzlingly bright. She struggles to find a space to stretch out her towel and, when she finds it, it's littered. Alessia picks up the ice cream wrapper and the discarded magazine. She will bin them on her way home.

She piles her clothes neatly by her towel, swaps sunglasses for goggles, and heads to the water.

Before diving in, she turns back to memorise

the view from the sea, so she can find her spot on her return. Thankfully, she thinks, her towel with cartoon fish is easily recognisable.

Alessia returns from her swim tired and cold. She finds her towel and lies down to warm up in the sun. She loves the feel of the sun on the skin of her back and soon she's thirsty.

She reaches out for her water bottle but her hand only clutches sand. Strange. She remembers putting her bottle there. Never mind.

She closes her eyes and is gently dozing off when, suddenly, something vibrates under her tummy.

She jumps and scrambles off the towel. She watches with alarm as the eye of a cartoon fish vibrates. A snake? Or a crab?

She yanks the towel and stares. It's a phone, vibrating inside a see-through plastic bag. She hasn't put it there and it's not her phone.

Neither are the clothes folded in a pile, nor the glasses on top of the clothes or the sneakers with the holes in the toes. Which means that this towel is probably not hers either. She's been lying on someone else's towel!

She steps back and covers the phone with the towel again. Then, embarrassed, she scuttles away.

***

Gregorio notices that something is wrong when he reaches for his glasses and finds a pair of sunglasses instead. He's lying belly down on his towel so he's a little disorientated. He sits up and looks around.

Where are his shoes? What's this pile of flowery clothes? The only thing he recognises is the towel. But when he runs his hand over the place where he's buried the phone, he finds nothing hard underneath—just soft sand.

He leaps to his feet. This is not his place and this is not his towel, he realises with embarrassment.

He glances over his shoulder, looking for the owner of this towel. Nobody is standing there, scowling at him. Gregorio leaves quickly and goes in search of his real towel.

He's owned it for almost twenty years and he had assumed there wasn't any other left in Palermo. Curiosity grips him. Who is the owner of the other towel?

By the time Gregorio reaches his actual towel, he can't get this question out of his head. He puts on his glasses and sets off in search of his towel-twin.

***

Alessia immediately notices that someone has been lying on her towel because he's left a man-shaped indent. Around the towel, the sand has kept the shape of his steps as he arrived and then left again, hurriedly.

He, too, must have got a shock, Alessia reflects with compassion.

She's about to shake any trace of the man off her towel and lie down on it when curiosity assails her. Who's this man who has kept his childhood towel for all these years like she has, and who isn't embarrassed of being seen at the beach with it?

Alessia would love to see him. She strolls nonchalantly back towards the other towel, glancing around casually. The owner hasn't come back yet so Alessia studies his things.

His sneakers have holes in the toes. He doesn't look after himself, she concludes. His stained T-shirt and frayed shorts confirm that he's yet another lazy slob.

But she's still curious to see him. She waits a while but he doesn't come. Alessia worries about leaving her stuff unattended, so she decides to stroll back and forth along the shore between the two towels, keeping an eye on both.

***

Gregorio has been swimming back and forward between the two towels, looking out for the owner of the other, but he still hasn't seen her.

He has strolled around the place and studied her clothes, her sandals and the magazine lying on her bag. The title of the magazine's content splashed on the cover—*Treat Them Mean, Keep Them Keen*—makes him think that this woman is one of the unkind and selfish ones. He really shouldn't give her any more of his time, but he's too curious to give up trying to see her.

He sits on the sand halfway between the two towels to keep an eye on both, pretending to sunbathe. He remains there even when the sun dips towards the horizon and the other beach goers start packing up and going home.

***

The sun is setting, the beach is emptying and Alessia is considering giving up and going home. But just as she's about to return to her place and pack up, a thought comes to her.

What if her towel-twin has had an accident? It's not normal to leave one's possessions unattended for so long! Perhaps the man is in difficulty out at sea.

Alessia rushes to the lifeguards' post and tells them that a man might be missing at sea.

The lifeguards are packing up too, but they stop and ask her question. Does she know where he's gone? How long ago? Can she describe him?

When it becomes clear that Alessia has no idea where the man has gone, she has never seen him nor does she know that he actually exists, they reassure her and continue shutting down their station.

Alessia feels silly. How ridiculous to wait all day for a stranger she knows nothing about!

Judging by the state of his clothes, he might well have abandoned them on purpose. As for his phone, he could have just forgotten it. Men can be careless like that.

Her shoulders are sore with too much sunshine. She should go home.

***

Common sense tells Gregorio that this is getting beyond ridiculous and he should go home at once.

The woman might well have gone home and forgotten her stuff behind. Anyway, he shouldn't be wasting his time over someone who reads articles like "Treat Them Mean, Keep Them Keen". Because of this stupid obsession with her, he's missed out on hours of swimming.

Gregorio decides to go for one last swim before heading home. The sea is warm and calm after a whole day of sunshine on the shallow waters. Now that the crowds have gone, he can swim freely, without fear of bumping into other bathers.

Suddenly, a sharp pain shoots up Gregorio's foot. He yelps, thrashes and another lash of pain strikes him in the arm this time. Gregorio yelps again. It's got to be a jellyfish! He leaps out of the water, hobbling on his stung foot.

A woman approaches him. "Are you okay?"

"Nothing serious. Just a jellyfish," Gregorio says.

"Ouch, that's very painful. I've got an ointment for it. I always take it with me when I go to the beach. Wait here," she says.

Gregorio watches her walk towards the towel with the fish and stop there. She's his towel-twin!

As she returns with the ointment and applies it gently on his stings, Gregorio's chest fills with a warm feeling he hasn't felt for a long time.

"Maybe it's better not to swim when the sun goes down. Have you just arrived at the beach?" she asks.

"No. I've been here for a while," he replies vaguely, unwilling to admit that he's been waiting all day to meet her. "What about you?"

"I've been here for a while too," she says shyly.

"I was just about to go for an ice cream," Gregorio improvises, hopeful to spend more time with her. "Can I offer you one?"

"That would be very nice. I'm Alessia, by the way."

"I'm Gregorio. I'll just go and grab my stuff."

***

Alessia watches Gregorio walk towards the fish towel and her heart makes a somersault. So he's the one she's been waiting to meet all day! He hadn't abandoned his stuff and left the beach after all.

She watches him shake the sand off his towel then fold it neatly. This is not the behaviour of a lazy slob.

"We have the same towel," she tells him when he rejoins her.

"I know." He blushes. "After my first swim of the day, I accidentally lay down on your towel instead of mine," he confesses.

Alessia chuckles. "I did the same to yours! It was only when your phone started ringing underneath that I realised the mistake."

Gregorio laughs, then pauses. "Do you always stay at the beach so long?"

"No," Alessia admits, touching her sun-sore shoulders. "How about you?"

"Me neither," he confesses. "I was too curious to see you to leave before that."

She chuckles. "Me too."

As they step onto the wooden decking, Alessia watches him dust the sand off his feet before putting on his shoes.

"Sand clogs up the vacuum cleaner," he explains.

Alessia is impressed that he's thought about that. He can't be a lazy slob, she reassures herself.

On the way to the ice cream shop, they walk past a refuse bin and Alessia drops the litter she had found on the beach.

"Aren't you keeping your magazine?" Gregorio asks, surprised.

"It's not mine. I found it littering the beach and picked it up," she explains.

"Of course. I should have guessed," Gregorio says with a satisfied smile.

7. GREAT EXPECTATIONS

"What trick are you going to play today, Giuseppe?" his classmate asked him.

When he was little, Giuseppe Sposito liked school. He loved wiping the blackboard and listening to stories of Ancient Egyptian mummies.

The problem was that his penwork was never good enough, and numbers had a habit of getting muddled up in the columns.

Giuseppe had repeated each class so many times that school seemed boring and pointless. At thirteen, he should be helping his dad in the shop, not sitting in a classroom with nine-year-olds.

"Quick, Maestra is coming!" the lookout warned him from the door, then shot back to his desk.

Giuseppe put a stick of chalk under each leg of the teacher's chair, and rushed to his seat.

"Good morning, Maestra!" the class

chorused, standing up.

Maestra Rocca walked into the classroom and climbed onto the dais. The children stifled giggles of anticipation.

"What's all this cheerfulness for?" she asked, then sat on her chair.

Bang! The chalk sticks shattered and the chair wobbled, scaring her.

"Giuseppe Sposito, stand in the corner!" she ordered.

He was already on his way. It was a well-rehearsed morning routine.

"Why can't you be more like the other Giuseppe?" Maestra asked, as she did every morning.

Giuseppe Abate, the best pupil in the class, grinned from the front row.

The naughty Giuseppe wished he could be like him, but that was never going to happen.

Today he had fulfilled expectations again.

***

Laura opened the envelope that Maestra Rocca had left for her. It contained a full class list with comments about each pupil.

When the bell rang, she had only reached Giuseppe Abate. Maestra Rocca described him as a trustworthy pupil she could rely on. That was all she needed to know. She closed the note and set off down the corridor.

Someone was looking out from the door of the classroom. It was a bad sign. This class was going to be hard work. In fact, when she stepped in, there was an air of mutiny.

"Where is our Maestra?" one of the girls enquired.

"She's not in school today. I'm substituting," Laura answered.

Murmurs rippled through the class. It was always like that. Children didn't like changes. They were creatures of habit.

She stepped onto the dais and was about to put her bag down on the teacher's desk. Suddenly, a boy who looked a lot older than the rest stepped forward.

"I wouldn't do that, miss. The desk is covered in glue."

She looked at the desk sideways. There was an almost imperceptible but unmistakable sheen. Someone must have had an accident with the glue. Thank goodness for that boy who had saved her and her favourite bag! He must be Giuseppe Abate, the one Maestra Rocca had written about.

"You are Giuseppe, aren't you?"

***

He shouldn't have told her about the glue. Giuseppe had exposed himself and now he was going to be punished.

Getting into trouble with his own teacher was fine. It was expected. He expected it, Maestra expected it, and everyone else in the class expected it. But being in trouble with someone new was a scary thing.

"Yes, I am," Giuseppe admitted sheepishly.

"Thank you for warning me." She looked into his eyes and smiled.

He blinked twice. Why wasn't she sending him to the corner?

"Could you please ask the janitor for a wet cloth, as you're such a good boy? Thank you."

He stood motionless. Teachers didn't say "please", "thank you" or call him a "good boy". Nor did they send him on errands out of the classroom. They feared that he might not come back.

"Could you, please?" she repeated.

He nodded vigorously and shot out the door.

When he saw him coming, the janitor frowned. "Where do you think you're going, young man?"

"The substitute teacher needs a wet cloth," Giuseppe told him.

When he returned to the classroom, he was asked to clean the desk, but it was clear that it wasn't a punishment.

It reminded him of when teachers still gave

him the privilege of wiping the blackboard. They used to trust him not to play with the duster.

Just as they had finished the lesson, there was a knock on the door.

"Our classroom is flooded. Can you fit us in?" the teacher from the class next door asked.

All the Year Ones filed in, carrying their chairs. Every Year Four was made to share their desk with each one of them.

There was one too many. Maestra Laura turned to Giuseppe.

"Please can you take two Year Ones with you?" she asked.

"Of course, Miss!" he agreed excitedly.

By the end of the day, Giuseppe had received so many compliments that, on the way home, he was walking on air.

***

Maestra Rocca trudged into the staffroom with a hollow feeling in her stomach. She dreaded to imagine how Giuseppe Sposito had behaved with the substitute teacher.

With trembling hands, she opened the note the poor woman had left her.

"Dear Maestra Rocca, your class has completed all the work you set. Thank you for letting me know that I could rely on Giuseppe. He has been a great help."

Maestra Rocca sauntered to her class with a smile on her lips. This time there was no lookout at the door to warn Giuseppe Sposito of her arrival. Surprisingly, he was sitting quietly at his desk.

"Well done for the good report I've received from the substitute teacher," she commented. She then looked at Giuseppe Abate. "A special congratulations goes to you. I hear that you have been especially helpful."

The boy was confused. "Maestra, I wasn't in school yesterday. I was ill."

Maestra Rocca frowned. If he wasn't in school, then who…?

"It was me!" Giuseppe Sposito called from the back of the class.

No, it was impossible. She fished the note out of her bag. It just said *Giuseppe*.

"Yes, it was him, Maestra," the class confirmed.

Giuseppe Sposito beamed.

Whatever had happened to him in her absence, it had to be a miracle.

"Well done, Giuseppe," she told him sincerely. "From now on I expect you to be a good boy. Do you think you can do it?"

"Of course," Giuseppe replied. "I always do what I'm expected to."

8. UNDER HER NOSE

Giovanna had made up her mind. It was time to find love.

She had achieved all her other life goals—a degree in engineering, a job in a reputable company and a flat of her own. Now it was time to find a husband and start a family.

She hadn't left this till last because she cared less about it, but because she had never known where to begin.

"There must be lots of single men at your work," her sister said when she asked for advice.

Giovanna agreed, but no sparks had ever flown there.

"Try online dating," her sister suggested.

Giovanna downloaded several apps, created a profile and scrolled through hundreds of potential matches. Overwhelmed by the choice, she deleted them all.

"I'm sure you can find someone at work. You just need them to see you as a woman, not just a colleague," her mum advised.

Giovanna let her mum take her shopping, to the hairdresser and to the nail salon. After the makeover, Giovanna admitted that she looked good—though not quite like herself.

When she walked into the office the next day, it turned out others didn't recognise her either. In her department, only her colleague Renato didn't do a double take.

At lunch, the canteen server asked for her badge. She'd left it at home, so Renato shared his lunch. But the worst moment was when she lost one of her acrylic nails in the ultracentrifuge.

Giovanna was disappointed. If a makeover wasn't the answer, what else could she try?

***

The answer came one bedtime, as Giovanna read her favourite science magazine. She sat up, eyes wide.

Apparently, people were attracted to genetically compatible partners through their natural scent and pheromones.

She glanced at the jasmine-scented perfume on her dresser. Of course! Men were drawn to women—not flowers!

She poured the bottle down the drain. From

now on, her only scent would be her natural pheromones!

***

Giovanna didn't usually go to the office gym but thought it might be worth a try. Vigorous exercise must release more pheromones.

She went straight after work, when the gym was busiest, and saw several eligible colleagues.

"Hi, Renato!" she called out.

Renato nearly dropped his dumbbells. "Hello. Sorry, I'm a bit sweaty," he said, reaching for a towel.

"It's fine," Giovanna said genuinely. He was doing exactly what she'd hoped—wafting pheromones.

They weren't bad.

"I've never seen you here," he said.

"It's my first time. Got any tips?"

Renato offered to show her around. As they moved from bench press to the leg press, Giovanna noticed his cheeks were still flushed. Was he okay? Did he have high blood pressure?

***

Giovanna kept up her gym visits for weeks, but no one showed the slightest interest in her pheromones. Since she wasn't keen on weights anyway, she gave up.

One afternoon, Renato appeared at her

desk. His was across the room; he had no reason to pass by.

"I haven't seen you at the gym. Are you all right?" he asked.

"I'm fine, thanks. I just decided to stop. My strategy wasn't working."

"What strategy?"

Giovanna told him about the article and her hope of attracting someone naturally.

"I don't think you need to worry about that," he said, his cheeks turning pink.

Was he unwell again? She worried for him.

"You should get your blood pressure checked," she said, ignoring the change of topic.

"Sorry?" Renato looked startled.

"I'll come to the GP with you, if you like," she offered.

Renato's face grew even redder. "I'd like to, er, go somewhere with you, but not to the GP," he said awkwardly.

Giovanna blinked. Did he mean a cardiologist? "Where else?"

"How about the cinema? Or lunch out—not in the work canteen," he clarified.

It finally dawned on her—he was asking her out! The redness wasn't illness—it was blushing.

"Yes, I'd like that very much," she said.

***

It didn't take Giovanna long to realise that Renato was the one. How had she missed him all this time?

Kind, generous and thoughtful, he ticked every box. And most importantly, his pheromones smelled amazing to her.

That's why, on their first month anniversary, she gave him a little gift.

He unwrapped it, puzzled. "A bottle of aftershave?"

Giovanna smiled.

"Just a precaution to stop you wafting those wonderful pheromones around other women."

They both laughed, then kissed.

9. THE LOCKED DOOR

Who had decided that "Blue Beard" was a story suitable for children? The story had haunted Simona as a child, and still upset her now that she was a grown-up children's writer.

But it wasn't her job to choose which stories would go into her publisher's "Classic Children's Tales" collection. Her job was to retell the stories in her own words and within the word count allowed by the illustrations.

She had done her best to make Charles Perrault's story as child friendly as possible. She left out the goriest bits, glossed over some details, and added rhyming verses with a jaunty rhythm.

But it was still the story of a murderer who hid the bodies of his wives in a locked room. When his new young wife couldn't resist her curiosity, she unlocked the forbidden door and dropped the key in the blood in her shock.

No matter how she tried to remove the stain

from the magical key, it wouldn't go. The poor girl looked set to end up like Blue Beard's previous wives, when her valiant brothers came to the rescue.

Was it a story about the importance of having devoted brothers? Of choosing one's spouse carefully?

Simona still had her doubts, but her publisher was expecting it, so she proofread it one last time, then hit *Send*. Now she could get ready for her date.

***

Federico had liked Simona from the moment they had been introduced. After that evening, they had met for coffees and dinners out, but tonight he had invited her to his place for the first time.

Making a good impression tonight was crucial. He had tidied and cleaned the flat, top to bottom. Now he had to cook to impress.

He opened the door to the flat adjoining his.

"Nonna, could you give me the recipe of your crème caramel?"

"Are you having visitors?" Nonna asked, looking out her sure-fire recipe.

"Yes, but don't worry, I'll lock the door between the flats. Nobody will disturb you."

"I don't mind, darling. You can introduce anyone to me," she said with a wink.

The truth was that it wasn't just for his nonna's sake that he wanted to lock the door. He didn't know Simona well enough yet to risk giving her the impression that he was one of those men who couldn't cook, clean or look after themselves.

In truth, Nonna and he were looking after each other. It was a mutual thing, and it worked very well, but a new girlfriend might be scared off. So he preferred to keep this conversation for later.

***

Federico's flat, in Palermo's historic centre, was within walking distance from Simona's, so she set off on foot.

Simona passed many beautiful buildings, and a plaque on an ancient house caught her attention.

Here, in 1734, was born Giuseppe Balsamo, also known as Count of Cagliostro.

The adventurer, alchemist and con artist had managed to pass himself off as an aristocrat and make his way into the European courts, tricking everyone along the way.

Thank goodness most men weren't like Cagliostro, or Blue Beard. And some were really very nice, like Federico. Usually the problem was in telling them apart.

***

She liked Federico's flat immediately. It was decorated tastefully, not minimalistic but not too cluttered. Another tick in his favour.

He had cooked delicious seafood pasta for their first course, braised sea bass for the second course, and a lovely lemony salad for a side. Another big tick.

All through the evening, the ticks in Federico's favour ratcheted up. By the time Simona left the table to use the toilet, she was very impressed with him.

She was in such a bubble of bliss that, when she got to the corridor, she had forgotten where he had told her the bathroom was. Was it the first on the left or the first on the right?

She didn't want to ask again and look stupid. She would just have to try all the doors until she found it. Anyway, she didn't mind an excuse to peek around the flat.

But when she tried the first door, it was locked.

Would she have thought anything of it if she hadn't been writing about Blue Beard all that afternoon?

A chill ran down her spine. Why was the room locked? He hadn't told her that he had a lodger. Was it always locked, or had it been locked only because she was coming? Crucially, what was inside?

She tried peeping through the keyhole, but she didn't see anything. She found the toilet and tried not to think about it. But it kept popping back into her mind, so when she returned to the table, she decided to ask Federico about it as casually as she could.

"I got the wrong door at first, but it was locked. What's in there?"

"It's just a storeroom," he replied, shifting his gaze.

Why had he said "just"? What more could it be? And why was he avoiding eye contact and hurrying to serve the pudding? He must be hiding something from her.

From then on, Simona was on edge. She memorised the route to the front door in case she needed to make a quick getaway. When she checked out an alternative escape route via the balcony, above the roofs of the other houses, she saw Cagliostro's birthplace. Was Federico a lovely boyfriend or a con artist?

She had to find out what was behind that door.

"Have we got any popcorn?" she asked him when they were getting ready to watch a movie on the sofa.

"Oh, I forgot it. If you wait here, I'll pop to the shop downstairs," Federico replied.

"Thanks."

He grabbed the keys to the front door from the key cabinet and rushed off.

This was Simona's chance to discover what was behind that door, but she had to act quickly.

Federico had left the key cabinet open. She just had to find the right key.

At her fifth attempt, the lock turned. With trembling fingers, she pressed the handle, pushed the door and froze.

It wasn't just a room on the other side—it was an entire flat. Images of Blue Beard and Cagliostro flashed across her mind.

The magazines on the coffee table told her that a woman lived in the flat. Federico evidently had a wife, maybe even children, and a whole secret life on the other side of the door!

"I'm back."

Federico's voice came from behind her, and she dropped the key on the floor.

***

It took Federico a couple of seconds to take things in. He watched Simona rush to pick up the key from the floor and rub it frantically against the leg of her jeans.

"I'm sorry—I can explain!" he exclaimed.

Wait—should he be the one to explain, or Simona, who had rummaged into his key cabinet and opened a locked door?

"Why didn't you tell me?" she asked, pale as the popcorn he was holding.

"I was afraid of losing you."

"But you can't have me if you've already got someone else!"

"I was hoping you two could get on well once you got to know each other."

Her features tightened. "There's space for only one woman in a relationship. I mean, how could you even imagine that—"

"Hello!" Nonna was coming towards them.

This was going to be very embarrassing.

"Who are you?" Simona looked confused.

"Nonna. This is my flat."

Simona burst into laughter and then tears, then hugged Nonna.

"I have never been so happy in my life!" she exclaimed.

Federico had no idea what was happening, but he was glad that Simona seemed to like Nonna.

***

Tonight was the first time Nonna was coming over with Federico to Simona's flat. Simona had cooked all afternoon, eager to make a good impression, but Nonna was impressed even before Simona had started serving the meal.

"You've written all these stories?" Nonna

asked, pointing to Simona's collection of children's books.

"The stories aren't mine, but the words are."

"I love fairy tales and folk tales, especially the ones where the old women are kind fairies," Nonna said.

"Me too," Simona agreed.

They exchanged opinions on many stories, and it turned out that Nonna knew even more stories than Simona did.

"I can't stand 'Blue Beard'," Nonna confessed.

Simona smiled. "I hate that one too. And, one day, I'll tell you a little story."

10. PUMPKINS EVERYWHERE!

Melina finished the last seam, cut the thread and pulled the cloth out of the sewing machine.

"Your costume is ready, love. Come and try it on."

Her five-year-old granddaughter, Valentina, ran to her with a grin and eyes full of sparkle.

"Thank you, Nonna!"

Tomorrow was the school's Halloween party and Valentina had asked for a skeleton costume. The hood framed her chubby little face perfectly and made her the poster girl for cuteness.

"You are the sweetest skeleton I've ever seen!" Melina exclaimed.

Just then, Tanino popped his head round the door. "Hello, ladies, what are you up to?"

"Nonno, look at what Nonna has made for me!" Valentina shouted, twirling around to show off her costume.

Tanino cocked his head. "What are you,

some sort of skeleton?" He shot a frowning glance at Melina.

"It's Valentina's Halloween costume. It's her school's party tomorrow," Melina explained.

A cloud shadowed Tanino's face. "I do not approve of this macabre feast. Witches and demons should not be celebrated," he said curtly.

Valentina might not have known what "macabre" meant, but she had certainly picked up on Tanino's tone and facial expression, because her little chin quivered.

Melina wrapped her in her arms. "Tanino, you're upsetting her!"

"And you, my dear wife, are leading her astray by encouraging her to take part in foreign pagan rituals. The other day I saw on TV that there are people, here in Italy, who do horrible things on—"

"We don't want to hear the details, Tanino."

She hugged Valentina tighter, as if to protect her from witches or demons.

"Tanino, you're making a mountain out of a molehill. The school party is just a little fun for the children."

But Tanino wasn't giving up.

"There are much better things to celebrate. Like the feast of All Souls' Day. Has anyone told you, Valentina, that on All Souls' Day the souls of our ancestors visit us and bring sweets and toys to the children who have prayed for them?"

Valentina's chin stopped trembling and her eyes lit up. "Like Halloween treats?"

Tanino groaned and ran a hand over his face. "No, it's nothing to do with Halloween. It's our own Sicilian tradition." He offered his hand to her. "Take off that skeleton costume and come with your nonno. I'll show you how we celebrate All Souls' Day here in Palermo."

Valentina wriggled out of her jumpsuit and rushed to take Tanino's hand. Melina watched them leave the flat, then folded the costume carefully. Wherever they were going, it would still be needed for the school party.

***

"When I was a little boy, children didn't get presents at Christmas. They didn't write letters to Father Christmas. Instead, children wrote to the souls of their ancestors and received presents on All Souls' Day. The night before, we put some food out on the table for the souls of the departed and the next morning we found a big basket full of sweet treats and presents," Tanino said, walking down the street with Valentina.

It had shocked him to the core to find out

that the child knew all about Halloween but nothing about the Sicilian way to celebrate All Souls' Day.

"What can the ancestors bring me? Do they have money?" the child asked.

"They can bring you anything," he said, stretching his arms grandly. "Well, so long as it doesn't cost too much. Sweet treats are their favourites."

The *pasticceria* shops were brimming with inexpensive sweets traditionally made for the festivity, and the seasonal market they were going to was bound to be full of them.

"You'll see them in a moment," he said, patting her hand against his leg.

He was going to introduce her to the marvels of the Sicilian All Souls' feast.

But when they got there, Tanino stared at the stalls in disbelief. What were all those fluorescent skeletons, fake blood-shot eyes and vampire teeth doing there? Oh, no, Halloween had spread here too!

"Nonno, can I have one?" Valentina asked, pointing to a row of glowing scythes.

"Ask your nonna," he answered curtly.

"Nonno, look, witches' clothes!" Valentina said as they passed by a stall overflowing with black and purple costumes.

"They are nothing to do with silly witches.

They are the clothes our ancestors used to wear," he lied.

He tightened his grip on Valentina's hand—all those skulls, skeletons and scythes disturbed him a little—and marched past those first stalls and dived deeper into the market.

Tucked into a quiet corner, away from the higher footfall of the main street, there was a long stall lit up by large dangling lights. Nuts of all shapes and kinds were spread over its length, basking under the lamps as if they were suns.

There were almonds and peanuts, walnuts and pistachios, hazelnuts and sunflower seeds. The traditional *calia*, toasted salted chickpeas, sat next to the *semenza*, toasted and salted pumpkin seeds. Tanino remembered eating tonnes of the stuff when he was little.

A hot, sugary smell came from the stand next to it, which belonged to the nougat man. He was using the longest knife to slice a flat, sticky cake cooking on a huge hot plate. Below it sat marzipan cakes in the shape of fruit, so well-crafted that they looked real.

"Look, Nonno, a doll!" Valentina pointed to a ballerina made of sugar.

There were also dolls of peasant women in traditional costumes, footballers in the colours of Palermo's team and *paladini* knights from the

Charlemagne legends that had been popular in Sicily for centuries. Their glossy white surfaces had been hand-painted with brilliant edible colours made with saffron, tomato, millet, cocoa and squid ink, and had been decorated with shiny strips of paper and ribbons.

"She's not just any old doll. All these figurines are made of sugar, can you believe it?" Tanino said.

"Can I have one?" she asked.

"Not today. Ask the ancestors' souls to bring you one, and you might receive it on All Souls' Day, if you've been good."

Valentina narrowed her eyes in the same way that her nonna did when she wasn't convinced. "It's not the ancestors who buy it. They don't have money in heaven. It's you, isn't it?"

"Oh, well…I give them a hand. One day, I will be an ancestor's soul too, and I will need your help to bring presents to your grandchildren."

Valentina thought about it, then smiled. "I will help you, Nonno. You can count on me."

Tanino felt tears prick in the back of his eyes. One day, Valentina would make sure that he, too, was remembered, and his descendants would get presents from him.

"So, which one of the sugar sculptures would you like from your great-grandparents?"

"That one," Valentina said resolutely, pointing to a sugar pumpkin.

The sugar artists, too, had buckled under the pressure of Halloween. Tanino felt totally deflated. At this rate, he stood more chance of being remembered by his great-grandchildren as a scary ghost than as a loving ancestor.

***

Melina heard the door open and rushed to it. What had Tanino and Valentina found at the All Souls' market?

Their gloomy faces and their empty hands were enough of an answer.

"Nonna, can you buy me one of the glowing scythes they sell at the market?" Valentina asked, pulling Melina's hand.

Oh, no, the market must have been full of Halloween goods, Melina realised.

Tanino kicked his shoes off and shuffled in his slippers to the sitting room, muttering under his breath.

"Nonna, can we go back to the market and buy it for tomorrow's party?" Valentina asked again.

Melina's gaze flitted between the sitting room, where Tanino was now watching TV at high volume, and Valentina. Tanino had clearly disapproved of the scythe, or he would have bought it then and there. He hated Halloween, but how could he ever hope to arrest the tide when even the school had embraced the feast?

"Yes, let's go to buy scythe, but we'll also buy something for your nonno. I've just had an idea but I need your help. Let's see what you think."

***

It was All Souls' Day. The sky was heavy with clouds and a chilly air seeped through the windows.

In the end, Tanino had gone back to the market and bought the ballerina sugar doll for Valentina because, before asking for the silly pumpkin, she had admired it. As she hadn't asked the ancestors for anything, the doll would just have to do.

Even if Valentina didn't care about the tradition of All Souls' Day and would probably let it drop before it got to the next generation, he felt it was his duty to carry it on.

Now he was going to the cemetery to freshen up the family's graves and fulfil that duty too.

The doorbell rang.

"Can you go?" Melina called out from the kitchen.

He padded to the door. There was nobody there. It must be one of those Halloween tricks…

Hold on. There was something on the doormat that looked very much like a treat rather than a trick.

It was a beautiful wicker basket overflowing with nuts, marzipan fruits and all the other Sicilian sweets for All Souls' Day. A proud sugar knight towered a good thirty centimetres above everything else, just like tradition dictated.

There must be a mistake, Tanino thought. Someone must have sent it to their neighbours, not them.

Tanino turned over the envelope that was jammed through the wickerwork and blinked. It read *Tanino.*

He rubbed his eyes and looked again. The letters were scrawled shakily, but they clearly spelled his name. He rushed back inside.

"Melina, Melina! Someone has sent me an All Souls' basket!" he shouted down the corridor.

"How nice. Who is it from?" she called from the kitchen.

Tanino stopped in the corridor. Should he open the card, or take the basket into the flat first? He decided to take the basket in first, because a sugar knight wouldn't be much protection against flesh-and-blood thieves.

Once the basket was taking its rightful pride

of place in the centre of the dining table, Tanino sat down with Melina and opened the card. It was a handwriting he recognised.

Souls of the ancestors who now have departed,
I know that you love us and are very kind-hearted.
Please, help me be good and, if it's not too big a bother,
give nice sweets and treats to my loving grandfather.
Valentina.

Tanino's eyes pricked with tears and he looked at Melina.

"I did help her to write it, but the words are hers."

Maybe, in years to come, he wouldn't be forgotten by his descendants after all. "Let's take this beauty to Valentina's place and share it with the family," he said, wiping his eyes with his sleeve.

"That's a great idea, because someone has got her hopes set on the sugar knight."

The End

Other books by Stefania Hartley

Collections of short stories:

Sicilian stories
A Quiet Life
To Be Loved
Sand, Sea and Tamburello
The Season to be Jolly
A Season of Goodwill
Drive Me Crazy
What's Yours is Mine
Stars Are Silver
A Slip of the Tongue
Confetti and Lemon Blossom
Fresh from the Sea

Community stories
Good Habits
Welcome to Quayside
Tales from the Parish

Keeping It Cool

Romance novellas:

How to Choose a Husband
The Italian Fake Date

Sweet Competition for Camillo's Café
Second Chances at Mamma's Trattoria
Under Far Eastern Skies

Cosy mysteries:
Father Roberto and the Missing Money
Father Roberto and the Runaway Ring
Father Roberto and the Rural Riots
Father Roberto and the Mystery of the Microscope
Father Roberto and the Commotion at the Catacombs

ABOUT THE AUTHOR

Stefania was born in Sicily and immediately started growing, but not very much. She left her sunny island after falling in love with an Englishman, and now she lives in the UK with her husband and their three children.

Having finally learnt English, she's enjoying it so much that she now writes novels and short stories which have been longlisted, shortlisted, commended, and won prizes.

If you have enjoyed these stories, please leave a review. To be the first to hear when she's releasing a new book, sign up for her newsletter and receive an exclusive short story: www.stefaniahartley.com/subscribe

www.ingramcontent.com/pod-product-compliance
Lightning Source LLC
LaVergne TN
LVHW020049110826
845155LV00029B/695

* 9 7 8 1 9 1 4 6 0 6 7 1 7 *